The Berenstain Bears'
TROUBLE WITH MONEY

When little bears spend
Every nickel and penny,
The trouble with money is—
They never have any!

A FIRST TIME BOOK®

The Berenstain Bears'
TROUBLE WITH

Random House 🏠 New York

Copyright © 1983 by Berenstains, Inc. All rights reserved under International and Pan-American Copyright Conventions. Published in the United States by Random House, Inc., New York, and simultaneously in Canada by Random House of Canada Limited, Toronto. *Library of Congress Cataloging in Publication Data:* Berenstain, Stan. The Berenstain bears' trouble with money. (First time books) SUMMARY: Brother and Sister Bear learn some important lessons about earning and spending money. [1. Money—Fiction. 2. Finance, Personal—Fiction. 3. Moneymaking projects—Fiction. 4. Bears—Fiction] I. Berenstain, Jan. II. Title. III. Series: Berenstain, Stan. First time books. PZ7.B4483Bfp 1983 [E] 83-3305 ISBN: 0-394-85917-0 (trade); 0-394-95917-5 (lib. bdg.) Manufactured in the United States of America

28

MONEY

Stan & Jan Berenstain

Brother Bear and Sister
Bear knew quite a lot about
the ways of Bear Country.

They knew where the most
beautiful wild flowers grew.

They knew where the wild berries were the thickest and juiciest.

They knew the best spot for watching sunrises . . .

and sunsets.

They knew where all the best honey trees were.

They even knew a very special place where you could almost always see a rainbow—from a secret space behind the waterfall.

But there were some things
they didn't know very much
about.

One of the things Brother and
Sister Bear didn't understand
very well was money.

Oh, they knew money was fun to have and even more fun to spend.
And whenever they got some—

as a present,

or for doing a chore for a neighbor,

or for no reason at all from Grizzly Gramps, who tended to spoil them,

or from Papa Bear, who spoiled them even more—

they ran as fast as their legs
could carry them to the Bear
Country Mall and spent it . . .

for honeycomb on a stick, a
balsawood glider that did loops,
a tiny little mouth organ that
only played three notes.

They never bought anything sensible, and they hardly ever saved. Once in a while Sister put money in her piggy bank. But she usually shook it out again before it had a chance to cool off from her hot little hand.

Brother didn't even have a piggy bank.

Mama was becoming concerned about the cubs' carefree, spendthrift way with money.

"I think Brother and Sister should have a regular allowance," she said one evening when she and Papa were working on the family books.

"An allowance!" said Papa.

"Yes, so they can learn to use money sensibly— to save, to plan ahead."

"Oh, no!" said Papa. "They're much too young for that sort of thing. Let them enjoy themselves! They'll have to worry about money soon enough when they're grownups," he added with a sigh.

But it was Papa who first lost patience with their carelessness about money.

It happened one day when the cubs had been at a mall spending some pennies a neighbor had given them for walking her dog.

That was when they saw the new video game. It was called Astro Bear and it looked very exciting.

ARCADE

"A video game! At the mall!"
Papa shouted. "You must think
I'm made of money!"
The cubs thought no such thing,
and when they pictured it, it
seemed very strange.

Mama could see that they were puzzled and she explained: " 'Made of money' is just a figure of speech, my dears."

That's when the cubs realized that the situation was serious. Because Papa Bear only used figures of speech when he was upset.

"You must think money grows on trees!" he shouted. Another figure of speech.

"Video games, indeed!" he continued, becoming more and more upset. "There was no such thing as video games when I was a cub! Why, I didn't know what money was until I was almost grown!"

"Precisely, my dear," interrupted Mama. "And that's why this might be a very good time to start Brother and Sister on a regular allowance, so they can—"

"Absolutely not!" roared Papa, knocking over a chair. "They must earn their money! That's what life is about—working, earning money, saving for a rainy day!"

The cubs knew how really serious the situation must be. Papa had used three figures of speech and knocked over a chair. They decided right then and there to mend their careless, spendthrift ways.

It turned out that the cubs were very good at earning money once they set their minds to it. First they gathered wild flowers from those special places they knew about. Then they made them into bouquets and sold them by the side of the road.

WILD FLOWERS 10¢ bu.

Business was very good.

They gathered those fat, juicy wild berries and sold them door-to-door.

Business was very, very good.

Brother and Sister were turning out to be even better at *making* money than they had been at spending it. They organized guided tours of Bear Country's finest beauty spots.

Sister's piggy bank was jammed full.

They started a very successful pet-minding service.

PET MINDING 10¢ AN HOUR

Brother had to borrow Mama's sugar bowl to keep the extra money in.

At first Papa was very impressed
and pleased. But when the cubs started
to sell maps showing the locations of
all the best honey trees, Papa began
to have doubts.

HONEY TREE
MAP
15¢

"Those honey trees are a family secret," he complained. "The cubs don't seem to understand that some things are more important than money.

"They've gone from caring too little about money to caring too much. Why, just look at them! They're turning into greedy, selfish little misers right before our eyes!" he continued. He pointed at the cubs, who did, indeed, look like little misers greedily counting their money.

"Cubs," said Papa in his sternest voice, "we're going to have to have another talk."

But before he could start his speech, the cubs took all the money they had earned selling flowers and berries, doing chores, minding pets, and selling honey-tree maps and dumped it on his lap.

"Here, Papa!" said Brother. "This is for you!"

"That's right," said Sister. "We thought if we made some money for you, you wouldn't have to worry about it so much. We hope it's enough."

Papa was so startled, and so em-barrassed at having been so wrong about them, that he was speechless.

"That's *very* generous!" said Mama. "It's quite a sum of money and I know Papa appreciates it. But I have what may be a better idea. Papa does worry about money, of course. Most mamas and papas do from time to time. But what Papa is really worried about is you. He wants to be sure you understand that there's more to know about money than how to spend it!"

"You know what I think?"
said Papa. "I think we should
start Brother and Sister on
a regular allowance so they
can learn to use money
sensibly—to save, to plan
ahead."

"An excellent idea!"
said Mama, smiling.

"What about the money we earned?" asked the cubs.
"You earned it, and it's yours," said Mama.
"What I suggest is that we take it down to the mall
and put it in the Bear Country Bank."
"Good suggestion," said Papa. "That money can be
your 'nest egg.'"

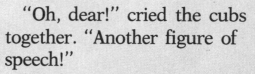

"Oh, dear!" cried the cubs together. "Another figure of speech!"

"And a very appropriate one," said Mama. She explained that the 'nest egg' is the one the farmer leaves in the nest to hatch another chick. "When you put money in the bank, it 'hatches' interest."

"Interest?" asked the cubs, puzzled.

"The bank will pay you for leaving your money there. That's called 'interest.' "

That day the Bear family went to the
bank and opened an account for the cubs.

It happened that the bank was right
next to the video arcade.

"Say, that looks interesting," said
Papa when he saw the Astro Bear game.
"Let's give it a try!"

So the Bear family gave Astro Bear
a try.

Papa ended up with the lowest score.
"You know," he said, "we didn't have
video games when I was a cub. Will you
give me another chance at this some-
time?"

"Any time at all!" said Brother and
Sister, giving their papa a great big
hug.